For Ste, with love,

xx

First U.S. edition 2018

Library of Congress Catalog Card Number pending
ISBN 978-0-7636-9626-9

17 18 19 20 21 22 GBL 10 9 8 7 6 5 4 3 2 1

Printed in Shenzhen, Guangdong, China

This book was typeset in Aldus.
The illustrations were done in watercolor, gouache, and pencil crayon.

Nosy Crow
an imprint of
Candlewick Press
99 Dover Street
Somerville, Massachusetts 02144

www.nosycrow.com
www.candlewick.com

Christine Pym

Little
MOUSE'S
BIG
BREAKFAST

nosy crow

An imprint of Candlewick Press

On a crisp cold day,
as the night crept in,
a hungry little mouse discovered
he had nothing to nibble for
breakfast the next morning.

He had searched every
sunflower for a seed
and every bush for a berry,
but **all** the food was gone.
There was **nothing** to
be found at home.

Luckily, Little Mouse
knew **just** where to go.

He scampered along the path . . .

up, up, up
the drainpipe . . .

until, finally,
Little Mouse . . .

hopped through an open window.

And there, on the table, was a bright blueberry.

Well, Little Mouse **loved** a bright blueberry.

A bright blueberry would be just
perfect for a little mouse's breakfast.

Little Mouse was just about to go home
when he spotted something else —

a rosy-red apple.

Well, Little Mouse **loved** a rosy-red apple!

A rosy-red apple would be
delicious with a bright blueberry
for a little mouse's breakfast.

But then, behind
the rosy-red apple,
Little Mouse
discovered . . .

some crunchy cookies!

And, behind the crunchy cookies, he found . . .

a chunk
of cheese . . .

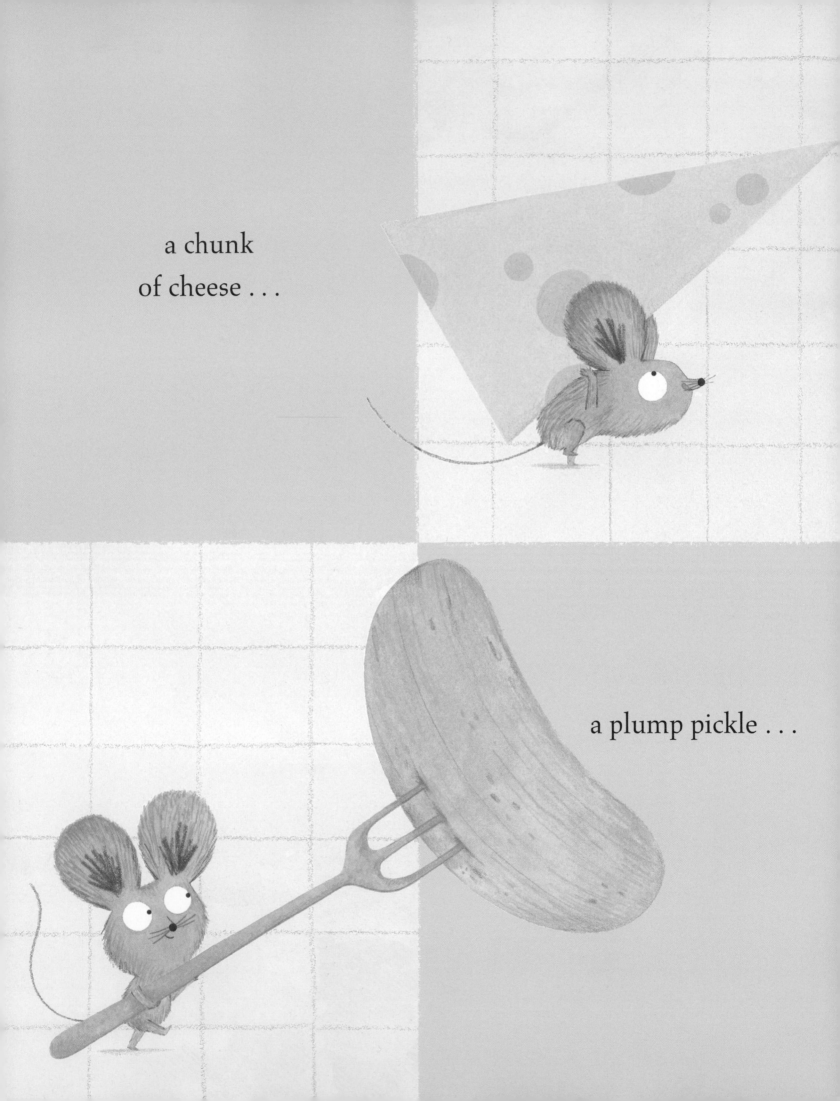

a plump pickle . . .

a spicy sausage . . .

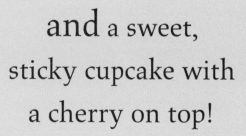

and a sweet,
sticky cupcake with
a cherry on top!

Little Mouse wasn't
sure if these things would
be particularly delicious,
but he decided to take
them anyway.

Little Mouse had **everything** balanced . . .

when he spotted something special . . .

something
very tasty . . .

something he **knew** would
be just **perfect** for breakfast!

A shiny striped
sunflower seed!

What luck!

Little Mouse loved a
shiny striped sunflower seed!
A shiny striped sunflower seed
was his favorite.

But just as he reached out to pick it up . . .

CRASH!

Little Mouse wasn't the only one looking for breakfast.

The big black cat **loved** a little mouse!
A little mouse was his **favorite**.

A little mouse
would be just
perfect for
a big black
cat's breakfast!

Luckily, Little Mouse
knew **exactly** what to do.

He hopped out
the window
and scampered . . .

down,

down,

down

the

drainpipe . . .

until, finally . . .

Little Mouse
was home!

And so, on a crisp cold morning,
Little Mouse had his first
bite of breakfast.

It was perfect.
But it was small . . .
and it was getting smaller. . . .

Little Mouse wasn't worried, though.
He knew just where to go. . . .